The Enchanted Weeping Willow

The Enchanted Weeping Willow

CYNTHIA JEAN DELUCA

Illustrated by Katie Dawe

ISBN: 9798467103464

My book is dedicated to all children who feel shy, bullied, and lonely.
Always remember how important you are! You are brave, strong, smart,
and caring! And you are loved, especially by me!

Cynthia Jean DeLuca

Table of Contents

CHAPTER ONE
Cindy and Her New Friend

The Enchanted Weeping Willow is a story about a lonely young girl named Cindy who desperately wanted a friend. Cindy grew up on a farm with her father, mother, two sisters, and one brother. Although her family did not have much money, she always had all the things she needed.

Cindy loved school but did not raise her hand even if she knew the answer. She was shy and afraid—afraid of saying the wrong thing, afraid other children would laugh and make fun of her. The girl did her work and followed the classroom rules but was very quiet. She was bullied and made fun of on the playground, in the lunchroom, and on the bus.

Then one summer, when she turned nine, the girl found a friend. Her new friend was tall with long, thin branches and tiny silvery-green leaves that almost touched the ground and swayed in the breeze. As she stood and looked at the tree she had seen many times before, something changed. It was as if the swaying branches were calling her, inviting her to walk through the curtain of leaves, where she could be anyone or anything she wanted to be without the fear of not being accepted.

"Mom, I finished my chores!" yelled Cindy as she grabbed a worn brown wicker basket filled with a handful of white drawing paper, a notebook, a pencil, markers, and her favorite book. In one hand, she carried her basket, and in the crook of her opposite arm, snuggled close to her side, were her blue blanket and green pillow.

She opened the old, squeaky screen door and walked barefoot through the green grass, down the little hill past her mother's brightly colored summer flower beds.

Cindy stopped and gazed at the tall weeping willow tree, whose branches were still as if the air had stopped. She sighed softly, thinking the branches reminded her of friendly, loving arms waiting to hug her. Cindy smiled, picturing each branch as a new friend waiting to laugh over something silly or draw beautiful pictures of cats with her.

CHAPTER TWO

Patches

Just then, a soft, sweet meow brought her back to the moment. She looked down and saw her black and white kitten, Patches, circling her feet. "Hello, Patches! I am so happy you could join me!" Cindy smiled, thinking back to the day when Patches was born. She was the tiniest kitten in the litter. Cindy remembered her heart melting as she watched the kitten try to find her way around, bumping into her brothers and sisters, making a slightly squeaky meow. She picked up Patches, held her close, and walked through the branches.

Cindy spread her blue blanket on the ground and then put her green pillow on top. She lay down, looking way up through the inside of the tree at the sun peeking down, jumping from leaf to leaf.

The sparkling flashes of light reminded her of the hundreds of lightning bugs that darted through the night sky. Cindy smiled as she thought about the fun she and her sisters and brother had every night when the evening sky turned from gray to black.

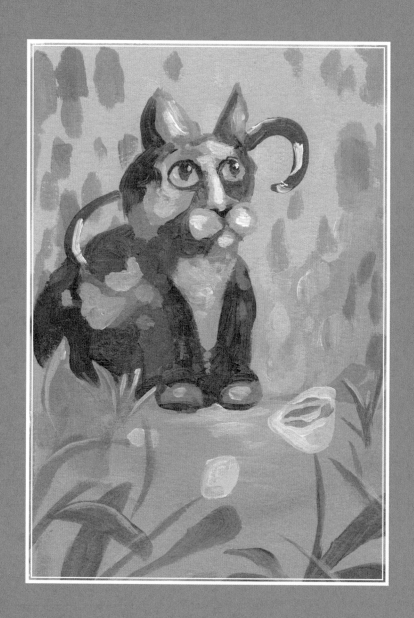

Oh, what fun they all had running through their big yard then, behind the barn, with small glass jars topped with lids dotted with holes, trying their best to catch the tiny flashing-yellow bugs. She sighed, thinking how fun it would be if she had a friend to catch lightning bugs with.

Cindy sat up, opened her notebook, and then wrote on the top of the page, "Catching Lightning Bugs with My Friend." She lay back down and looked for a long time at Patches, curled up by her side. She smiled, listening to the sounds of soft purrs, closed her eyes, and told her sleepy kitty this story.

CHAPTER THREE

Superheroes

"Once upon a time, a lonely girl wanted a friend, a real friend who loved trees as much as she did. Someone who liked to draw, read, sing, dance, and laugh. Someone who would not make fun of her when she was quiet." She paused for a moment and said, "Patches, if I am lonely there must be other kids who are lonely, too."

Then, in a flash, Cindy said, "Patches, today we are going to go on an adventure." Cindy thought some more and then continued, "I think we will look like birds, flying high over tall mountains, through dark green forests, and then down over oceans and rivers."

Patches looked up at Cindy, not caring whether they looked like birds or how far they would fly as long as they were together. Just then, like a light bulb going off, Cindy said, "Everyone needs a hero. Especially boys and girls who are lonely. Patches, I wish I could be a superhero. And with that, she fell fast asleep.

Patches felt Cindy stirring and then watched her sit up and rub her eyes. Both of them walked through the long branches into the sunlight. Outside, Cindy felt different. She felt stronger. Then she looked down and could not believe her eyes! She was no longer wearing everyday clothes. Instead, she was dressed in a pink bodysuit with a flower stamped on the front. A darker-pink cape was attached to her shoulders, and glasses that matched her cape framed her face and completed her outfit. She thought, *If only the kids at school could see me now.*

Cindy looked over at Patches, and her eyes grew as large as saucers. Patches had a giant pair of yellow glasses sitting on top of her nose! Cindy stood there for a few minutes and then looked at Patches and said, "Patches, it's time for our adventure—are you ready?" Patches purred as if to say, "Up, up, and away!" With Patches sitting on her shoulder, Cindy put her arms straight up in the air, and instantly she was flying high and then higher over tall mountains, lakes, and rivers. The superheroes were on their way to find lonely children. Patches patted Cindy's shoulder once then twice. "What is it, Patches? Do you hear something?" Then Cindy heard someone talking softly.

Suddenly, Cindy and Patches flew over a grove of tall green evergreens. She had to get a closer look. Cindy's arms pointed downward, and then she and Patches followed the soft voice.

They landed near a patch of flowers. The pink flowers reminded Cindy of the one on the front of her superhero suit. Then, as they walked around a large evergreen tree, Cindy spotted a boy around her age sitting next to a small brown dog. She told him not to be afraid—she was a friend.

The superheroes sat down next to the boy and listened to his story. His name was Danny, and he lived on a small farm nearby. His parents worked hard but did have a lot of money. The kids at school made fun of him and never picked him to play a game or be on their team. It sounded just like her story.

Cindy listened some more. Then she told the boy about her weeping willow tree and how she could be anyone she wanted to be. Cindy asked the boy what his favorite thing was to do. He smiled and answered, "I have many things I like to do, like drawing pictures and reading books. Oh, yes, I love to sing!" Cindy asked him what his favorite song was. He answered, "All of them!" Under the tree, the superhero and the boy sang song after song while Patches and the brown dog curled up and took a nap.

Then the boy disappeared. As the superheroes were getting ready to fly again, the boy ran after them, shouting, "Wait, please wait! These are for you." He handed Cindy one pink flower and said, "Thank you! I want to be your friend."

Cindy took the flower, smiled, and said, "Thank you for the flower. I will always be your friend. When you are lonely, think of me."

The superheroes flew up into the air again and searched for more voices. They found several more girls and boys. Cindy and Patches listened to their stories and promised always to be their friends.

Patches licked Cindy's face until she woke up. She rubbed her eyes and looked at her dear friend. "Patches, I have so much to tell you! I was dressed in a pink superhero outfit, and you had on big yellow glasses. We flew everywhere and found so many lonely kids—kids that needed a friend." Patches looked at Cindy and purred; it almost sounded like, "You will always be my superhero."

That afternoon, Cindy shared her superhero story with her mom. After Cindy left the room, her mother smiled and thought, *That girl sure has a wild imagination.* That night, Cindy drew a picture. The picture was of her and Patches dressed up like superheroes. Underneath the picture she wrote, "Super Friends."

Super Friends

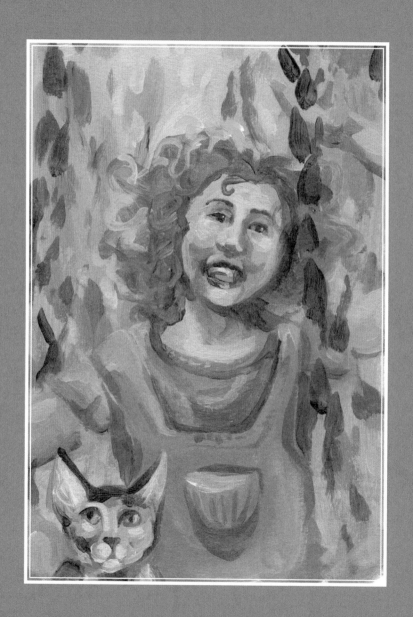

CHAPTER FOUR
Dancing with the Willow

The next day, Cindy finished her farm chores early and hurried down to her tree. Patches was waiting for her by the long branches with the soft green oval leaves. Cindy had her basket filled with everything she needed to be cozy underneath the cool shade of the branches.

"Did you know that I love to sing and dance?" Patches purred as she watched Cindy stand up and sing at the top of her lungs. She purred some more as Cindy sang song after song. Then Cindy took ahold of six branches, three in each hand, and danced with her tree! She danced and danced. Patches stood up, flicked her tail, then moved her head from side to side. Cindy giggled as Patches kept flicking her tail, then sat down on her blue blanket to catch her breath.

CHAPTER FIVE
Kite Flying

The next day it rained and rained. Cindy could hear the wind blowing, almost howling like a coyote. She held Patches in her arms as she looked out her bedroom window. The long branches on the weeping willow were flying high, then low, and sometimes straight out. It reminded Cindy of a kite flying high in the sky.

That afternoon while Patches was curled up and taking a nap, she drew a picture of a yellow kite with a tail of oval green leaves. Patches purred as if to say, "It looks great!"

Rainy days were hard for Cindy. She thought if she only had a friend, they could paint pictures together. They would paint lots of kites then pretend to fly them all around her room – or maybe around the world.

CHAPTER 6
How to Be a Friend

The sun was shining the following day as Cindy helped her mother in the kitchen. They were going to make chocolate chip cookies for a family picnic. As Cindy mixed the butter and sugar for the soft cookie dough, she glanced at the calendar with the trail of *XX*'s leading up to the first day of school. She wished she had more time to spend under her tree with Patches. Cindy sighed at the many stories she had yet to tell Patches and the pictures she wanted to draw and hang on the thin branches. (Picture 7)

As her mother mixed the flour, salt, and baking soda, she asked Cindy if she would like to go school shopping for a few new outfits and a pair of new shoes. Cindy softly answered, "Mom, you can shop for me. It's okay." Her mom looked at her, wiped her floured hands on her white apron with its tiny pink flowers, then walked over and gave Cindy a big bear hug. (Picture 8)

"Cindy, I know that you're lonely and would like a friend. Always remember that to have a friend, you must be a friend."

"Mom, they make fun of me. They call me Farm Girl. I'm always the last to be picked for the relay races. It hurts my heart," replied Cindy with tears in her eyes.

"Honey, this is a brand-new school year. You have to give your classmates a chance to see the real Cindy."

"Mom, you don't understand. I am afraid that I'll say the wrong thing or that my words will get mixed up and come out jumbled. It happens every year on the first day of school," replied Cindy as she pleaded her case, feeling hopeless.

"I know how much that hurts your heart, Cindy, but it might help if you learned ways to show everyone who you are. I hear you telling stories to Patches and singing all the time. I listen when you talk to the animals in the barn. And the dancing! You have a kind heart, and you are funny and talented. You love to read and have an incredible imagination. Cindy, you need to show them that you are not afraid. Your classmates are not going to bite you.

"Keep trying, Cindy. One kind word would be a great way to start. Remember, one word leads to another and another, and if you keep trying and don't give up, before you know it, you will have many friends." Cindy wanted to believe her mom, yet the fear she felt held her back. Her mom was quiet for a few minutes and then said, "Cindy, you have been telling me all about the stories you read since you learned how to read. I always loved how your expression changed and the excitement I heard in your voice when you told me your favorite part of the book. You always looked me in the eye to make sure I was listening. How about if we practice keeping your head up, introducing yourself, and responding when one of your classmates is talking to you? We can even practice raising your hand when you know an answer to a question. What do you think?"

Cindy answered, "I'll think about it, Mom."

CHAPTER SEVEN
Chatting with Patches

After the picnic, Cindy picked up her basket and headed down to her tree. Patches was curled up on the front porch, taking a late – afternoon nap when one of her eyes jerked open, as she heard the branches of the weeping willow swishing back and forth.

As Patches walked down the hill, she could hear Cindy's voice. Her voice got louder the closer Patches got to the tree. Patches wondered what was going on. Cindy looked up from her book when she saw Patches peeking through the branches.

"Hello, sleepyhead! Glad you could join me!" Cindy placed the bookmark in her book and pulled Patches onto her lap. "School begins in two weeks, and I am already starting to feel butterflies in my stomach. Mom said I should be brave and keep trying. Oh, how I wish you could talk to me and help me to figure this all out." Patches looked into Cindy's eyes and purred and purred. It almost sounded like, "You are the bravest girl I know. You got this." (Picture 9)

Cindy smiled, then picked up her mystery book, a Nancy Drew adventure—her favorite.

It was starting to get a little dark when Cindy heard her mom calling her. She quickly picked up everything from under the tree and headed up the little hill with Patches following close behind.

For the next two weeks, Cindy and her mom practiced and practiced what to say, like "Hi, I'm Cindy." She practiced looking in her mom's eyes as she spoke. When her mom said something silly, she practiced a little laugh. She practiced and practiced until the little laugh became a real laugh, a big laugh, so big that her mom laughed too. Cindy practiced raising her hand when she and her mom played school. She was starting to feel a little better about the first day of school.

Headed down to her tree, Cindy carried her basket filled to the brim with her favorite books and everything she needed to draw her pictures and write stories. Each day, she told Patches all about what she and Mom had practiced. Patches looked at her dear friend and purred a sweet meow of approval.

Cindy told Patches how she hoped that fourth grade would be different. Patches listened and purred messages of "You can do this. I believe in you!"

CHAPTER EIGHT
The First Day of School

After the two weeks, Cindy felt better about herself. She had worked hard with Mom and even practiced with her dad. She had decided that she would be the best person she could be. She would smile more, talk more, and help more. Cindy was ready to find a new friend – that is until the first day of school arrived – along with the feeling of hundreds of butterflies fluttering in her stomach.

Cindy had gotten up extra – early to get ready for school. Her mother had bought her a pretty dark-green dress with tiny pink flowers with yellow centers. She loved it. Next, she put on her pink socks and new black-and-white saddle shoes. As Cindy looked in the mirror, she smiled. Even her frizzy hair looked tamed. Then, like the superhero in her dream, she felt stronger, ready to fly high, ready to find someone who liked to do the things she enjoyed.

As Cindy walked into the school and then down the hall to her classroom, her heart started to race. Her mind was racing too. Would her new friend be waiting for her?

Would she be afraid to speak her name like she used to be, or would she be strong and brave like she knew she could be now?

Then, as she walked through the fourth-grade classroom door, the sadness she had worked so hard to chase away came rushing back like waves crashing onto a sandy shore. Cindy heard familiar voices, saw familiar faces, and knew that her classmates were the same as they were in third grade. There were no new students in her room. Finding a new friend was definitely not going to happen this year. Then she remembered what her mom said: "To have a friend, you must be a friend." Cindy thought to herself, *Okay, Mom, I will try for one week to be a good friend*

CHAPTER NINE
Friendship

Mrs. Lily welcomed everyone to fourth grade and asked them to move their desks into a circle. She sat in the circle too. Then she read a book about the first day of school. After she finished the story, she wrote, "Friendship" on the whiteboard with a green marker. "Boys and girls, what does friendship mean to you?" Everyone was quiet. No one raised their hand.

Cindy looked around the room and then slowly raised her hand. She thought she heard a giggle and quickly put her hand down. Mrs. Lily, smiling, said, "It's okay, Cindy. Please share what friendship means to you."

Cindy looked down at her desk and softly said, "When you are a friend, you are kind to everyone."

CHAPTER TEN
Brave and Confident

Mrs. Lily smiled again and thanked her for sharing. However, Cindy had more to say.

"To have a friend, you must be a friend. You need to be kind and care about others. When you play a game, it is important to include everyone. It should not matter where you live or if you have a lot of clothes. Or if you have frizzy red hair. Friendship means respecting other people's opinions and feelings."

Mrs. Lily walked over to Cindy and gave her a hug. "Thank you, Cindy! You were very brave to share your feelings with us."

Then something wonderful happened. Everyone clapped for her. Cindy smiled, and her heart felt as bright as the sun shining on a summer day. As the morning went on, Cindy raised her hand again and again. At lunchtime, two girls asked her to sit with them. Of course, she said yes.

At the end of the day, Mrs. Lily asked each of her students to share a little something about themselves. Cindy raised her hand up high and said, "I love living on our farm, and I love all the animals, especially my cat, Patches. She is my best friend. On our farm there is a special place where I can be anyone or anything I want to be." Cindy stopped before she shared her special place. She was afraid her classmates would laugh.

Then Bill, who had teased her last year, raised his hand and asked her where her special place was.

Cindy felt a little frightened, but Mrs. Lily encouraged her to share with a nod. Cindy looked around the room, smiled, took a deep breath, and said, "My special place is under a tall weeping willow tree with long branches and soft green oval leaves that almost touch the ground."

Cindy held her breath, waiting—but instead of laughter, she heard many of her classmates say, "Wow!" However, for Cindy, the best part was when ten of her classmates raised their hands and shared their special places.

As Mrs. Lily's class waited for their buses, two girls asked if they could come to her farm to see her special tree. Cindy smiled and said she would ask her mom and dad.

On the ride home, Cindy thought about her first day in fourth grade. It was a good day. A happy day. A day she would always remember. This was the year she had been waiting for. A year she would have a friend. In fact, more than one—many, just as her mom had told her.

As her yellow school bus pulled up near her mailbox, Cindy glanced out the window and spotted her mother. She smiled and got off the bus, and then gave her mom a big hug and said, " Thank you!" Cindy put her backpack down, picked up Patches, and then walked down to her tree. She could not wait to share her first day of school with her two best friends.

A Message from the Author

Dear boys and girls,

Hello, it's nice to meet you! My name is Cynthia Jean DeLuca, the author of *The Enchanted Weeping Willow*. I am the little girl, Cindy, in the book. Although a small portion of the book is fiction, it is my story. I was that shy little girl who would not raise her hand in the classroom or talk to her classmates for fear of making a mistake or having her words come out wrong. I was the little girl who desperately wanted a friend. The weeping willow, with its long branches and silvery-green oval leaves, sat at the bottom of a little hill in our backyard. My cat, Patches, and I shared many summer days under that tree, where I could be anyone or anything I wanted to be. With the help of my mother and the love I felt from Patches, I was able to become confident and believe in myself.

If you are shy, practice what you would like to say to your classmates. If you are bullied, ask your teacher to help you. Always remember, you are strong, brave, and loved.

Your friend,
Cynthia Jean DeLuca

Made in the USA
Middletown, DE
09 December 2021

54866020R00027